FORAGER

STEVE SWARINGEN

Forager

Cover Photo by Fabrizio Conti on Unsplash

Author Photo © 2017 Sarah Harigan Photography

Spears & Cornelius Publishing
Entertain. Educate. Inspire.

To you,
the ardent reader,
the inquisitive learner,
the introspective intellectual,
the passionate thinker.
That rare soul who actually bothers to read the dedication.
Enjoy.

Reconnaissance

Mabel watched as the alien star rose over the horizon of the planet below. Morning sun reflected from dense clouds as a winter storm moved slowly over the continent. It was difficult to see where the tempest ended as white clouds gave way to white snowpack.

The people below would have said the view was breathtaking. For Mabel, it was just doing her job—a job she'd been doing twenty-four-and-a-half hours a day for more than four months.

She switched to infrared wavelengths where she could easily distinguish the clouds. The storm had moved beyond their encampment, but heavy snow blanketed them. They would want to see this.

An incoming message interrupted her task for a tiny fraction of a second. As she acknowledged the request, she resumed surveying the planet's surface and began uploading the last eight hours of recorded data.

It never occurred to Mabel to wonder what it was like for the people below. How would it feel to wake up with two feet of snow covering your camp? To hear blizzard-force winds blowing in the darkness the night before? To watch as structures and equipment critical to your survival are destroyed by the gale? To be eight people marooned on an alien world with no way to get home and no way of knowing when—or even if—home would be coming back for you?

How would it feel to be human?

Mabel would never know. Mabel would never wonder.

Reset

Alex Guerrero wouldn't admit it, but he was cold. Working outside for more than four hours in blizzard conditions had chilled him to the bone.

Not having the right equipment didn't help. They hadn't come prepared for this kind of weather. He was wearing a light jacket and thin Kevlar gloves, with a towel wrapped around his head and face, leaving a narrow slit so he could see. But he had endured far worse conditions on other deployments.

And he finished the job. It would never occur to him that there might be another option.

"Close that door!" Culpepper shouted. "What, were you raised in a barn?"

Guerrero shut the door and shook the last of the snow from his jacket and gloves. "Ahhh. Nothing like a light workout and a little fresh air to get your day started on the right foot."

Steadman, who had already started taking off his own snow-covered outer garments, gave Guerrero a warning glare. Commander Chris Steadman was Alex's commanding officer and the other Navy SEAL assigned to the team for force protection. Most of the rest, like Culpepper, were scientists.

Teri Culpepper huddled her athletic frame in front of the heater vent, still trying to get warm after her own short effort. The rest of the team sat on chairs or beds arrayed around the perimeter of the room.

The medical lab had become their *de facto* gathering place. The two crew quarters buildings were partitioned in a way that didn't facilitate having everyone in the same room. The storage building was packed full of supplies and kept cold to preserve the food they had put away to get them through winter. The science lab was home to too much active research to accommodate interlopers.

"Status?" asked Decker, the mission commander. He was career navy, the last five years as the captain of a reconnaissance submarine.

"I just finished reviewing the latest satellite data from Mabel," said Swenson, the team's civilian engineer. "The storm has passed, and we're covered in snow. In case anyone didn't already know that. It does look like we shouldn't have any more big storms, at least for the next few days."

Culpepper shivered.

Steadman glanced at her and shook his head. "The greenhouse is gone," he said. "Everything we can find has been collected and stored. Unfortunately, that's not much. More than half of the wood used for framing is not much better than firewood now. What plastic

4

sheeting didn't blow away is shredded in pieces too small to be useful. We collected what plants we could and put them in the portal where they can be kept warm. Dr. Culpepper will have to assess the damage there."

Decker looked at Culpepper. "Doctor?"

Over the course of the three months they had been stranded here together much of the formality in their relationships had fallen aside. Dr. Culpepper was the lone exception. She still insisted on being addressed by her title.

She turned around to face the rest of the team, sitting on the floor in front of the vent—and blocking its warmth from everyone else. "It's a total loss. I might be able to nurse a few plants back to health, but any hope of them producing useful quantities of food during the next few months is gone. We're in for a rough winter."

"Grace?"

Dr. Grace Tornquist, the team's medical doctor, looked around the room at the others. "It's not good, but we'll survive. We have enough in stores that the next few weeks won't be a problem. There's still plenty of wild game in the area to provide protein and fat. We'll run out of carbohydrates, but we should be able to compensate with an increased protein intake. Vitamins are the big problem. General health will begin to deteriorate once our supply of fruits and vegetables runs out. We'll be more susceptible to illness, less able to recover from injury or exertion."

"Rationing?" Decker asked.

Tornquist shook her head. "I still have work to do to finish updating the plan, but what I just laid out already assumes optimal stretching of our remaining reserves. I should also point out that this assumes a lot of things we don't know. We have two months of supplies at minimally acceptable nutritional intake levels. We guess that we still have three months of winter, and then at least a couple of months after that before spring produces enough of the right vegetation to fill those gaps. Dr. Culpepper thinks it could take much longer before some of the fruits we need produce."

Decker looked around at his team. "Options?"

"I'm continuing to work through the backlog of nutritional analyses," Culpepper said. "There's nothing left out there that we'd normally think of as food, but we might get lucky. It's a longshot."

Guerrero looked around the room. Eight people huddled in a box trying to keep out the cold. This wasn't the plan. His job was to keep everyone safe, to make sure they all made it home alive. They had been ten; now they were eight. That was on him. This was on him. Setting all the positive attitude aside, not everyone would survive the winter ahead if they stayed on this path. There had to be another way.

He looked at Culpepper. "What about the southern hemisphere?"

Rethink

Culpepper stared out the window of the vehicle as they cruised a thousand feet above the crests of the canyons. The view was spectacular. Steep canyon walls striped in varied earth tones with a mostly dry streamed in the bottom. Small patches of several different types of cactus sparsely dotted the landscape. Beautiful, but useless. Nothing in sight that would help them survive. No good reason to land the four-wheeler here.

Their conveyance was somewhat paradoxical. They had begun referring to it as a four-wheeler not because it had four wheels but because it could go anywhere. Almost literally. It looked like someone had taken an extended-cab short-bed pickup truck from the assembly line before the powertrain was added. It had wheel-wells, but no wheels; an engine compartment, but no engine—at least not in the traditional sense. These had been replaced by a power source and propulsion system invented by the same man who had created the transit portal that brought them to this planet. No one here knew how either technology worked. Nor did they understand why the transit portal had stopped working, leaving them stranded fifty-seven light years from Earth.

This was a bad idea. I told them this was a bad idea. Did they listen to me? Noooo. "You'll make a good team." Good team. Right. The botanist and the meathead.

A metallic click broke her reverie. "Are you cleaning that gun again! You just cleaned it yesterday. And the day before that."

"And the day before that, and the day before that," Guerrero said. "A craftsman treats his tools with respect. On the subject of which, that tablet will serve you longer if you'll stop smacking it against the dashboard."

"I can't concentrate when you're doing ..." she waved her tablet at his disassembled rifle, "that."

"You can always find a distraction when you're looking for one."

She shifted in the seat to face him. "What, exactly, is that supposed to mean."

He snapped the barrel of his rifle back into place. "It means you've been cooped up in the cab of a pickup truck for three days with nothing to do but stare at snow-covered mountains and desert plains as we sail over them at a thousand feet."

"I'm *trying* to review these nutritional analyses."

Guerrero put his reassembled rifle to his shoulder and sighted down the barrel as he pointed it at the floor between his feet. "Dr. Tornquist has already reviewed that data and didn't find anything useful. Granted, you're the expert. But you know she knows what she's doing. If there were any prospect of anything good, she would've flagged it. You're looking for a distraction. So am I. That's why I'm cleaning my rifle. Again. It relaxes me— helps me think."

"Hmph. Don't strain yourself." Culpepper shifted back around in her seat, looking again at her tablet. "Stick to your strengths."

He cycled the action on his rifle. "That's why I'm here."

Is there a way for you to not be here?

She was just beginning to get back in the zone when Decker's voice came over the radio.

"Forager, this is Beachhead. How do you hear?"

Her focus lost yet again, she rapped her tablet against her forehead. *Can you not at least talk in complete sentences?*

Guerrero responded, "Beachhead, Forager. Loud and clear."

"How's your progress?"

He consulted the autopilot display. "We're a few miles ahead of schedule. Probably had a tailwind last night. Power consumption is right on target. We should arrive at the first objective early tomorrow morning."

"Roger. The drone should be on location by now. Our communication window with it will open in a few minutes. We probably won't have time to do much analysis before our window with you closes in the next hour, but we should have good data for you by this evening. Swenson is recommending you slow your approach to conserve power. There's no point in rushing to get there before sunrise."

"Wilco. Over."

"Beachhead out."

Culpepper looked out the window again at the terrain zipping by below them.

Another day yet. At least I'll have something to do once we get there. And then the trip back. Ugh.

Savanna gradually replaced the canyons.

Maybe I can walk back. I wonder how long it would take to walk six thousand miles? Might be worth it.

"Find a place to set down," she said.

He looked at the terrain map. "Here? Let's keep going. We're making good time. We can stop in another hour or so."

"Now! I need to stretch my legs. Decker said we needed to slow down anyway. It's not going to make us late to stop here for a few minutes."

Respite

Yes Ma'am. Set it down now.

Alex Guerrero took the four-wheeler off autopilot and nosed down toward the ground. The scrub trees were sparse enough that, in a pinch, he could set down almost anywhere. But, whether Culpepper liked it or not, that wasn't the way this worked. They were more than four thousand miles from their base camp, in a part of the world they'd never explored, on a planet they'd been on for less than three months, and with no drones to monitor their perimeter.

These stops were necessary, but the riskiest part of the mission. In the air, they had almost unlimited visibility and were out of reach of anything that could do them harm. There were still too many unknowns on the ground, especially now that they'd moved well away from their base camp.

He spotted a small clearing up ahead and angled toward it. Slowing his approach, he made a broad circle around the perimeter to give the four-wheeler's cameras a good look at their surroundings.

"Horses!" she said.

The computer watched for anything in motion. Culpepper's job on approach was to assess anything it flagged while Guerrero concentrated on navigation.

He centered up over the clearing but didn't land. "Where?"

Culpepper pointed past him out the left window. "There!"

He spotted about two dozen animals that looked like Earth horses scattered about among the trees. Most were grazing, but several had turned to look up at them as they hovered twenty feet off the ground.

Big. Fast. We're outnumbered and on their turf. Guerrero took the controls and started pulling out.

"Set it down. Horses are herbivores, they're not territorial, and rarely aggressive unless threatened. If there were any real threats here, *they* wouldn't be here."

He looked at her. *Makes sense. But then, these are not Earth horses.* He looked back over his shoulder at the herd. When the four-wheeler pulled out, most of them had returned to grazing.

Guerrero turned the vehicle around and brought it in for a landing, being careful to take a slow approach from a direction that would minimize the perception of threat to the animals.

He looked out his window. "Let's take this slow. Give them a chance—"

The sound of Culpepper's door opening interrupted him. He spun his head around and saw her jump out of the vehicle, sling her pack over her shoulder, and take off at a trot toward the tree line in the direction opposite the herd.

"Where are you going!"

"The ladies' room," she shouted. "The little boy's room is over there." She pointed back over her shoulder in the direction of the horses. Most of whom, he noted, were now looking directly at him.

Stretch your legs. Sure.

Regulations

Culpepper watched out the window as Guerrero brought the vehicle to a hover over a large clearing. The sun was just beginning to peek over the treetops to the east. In the dim light of dawn, she could see orange and green fruits covering the trees beyond the clearing.

I hope today's results are better than yesterday's.

They had visited four locations in the last six days. Two of those had yielded nothing useful. Perhaps a month earlier or a month later, things might have been different, but nothing that was ripe now and suitable for human consumption. They'd found good options at the other two stops, and in each case had stayed an extra day to harvest what they could. But there were still critical nutrients they had to find if they were going to survive the winter. So they kept moving.

A survey drone hovered a hundred feet to their north over another patch of the same clearing. That would mark where Swenson wanted the transponder set for the portal. They had been through the same drill yesterday and the day before: touch down at sunrise; collect as many different samples of fruit and vegetation as they could before Mabel passed overhead and the communication window opened; set the transponder and pack their produce tightly around it; say the word and watch it disappear, leaving a divot ten feet in diameter and two feet deep in the turf.

Swenson, the team's civilian engineer, would lock onto the transponder as a location reference and use the portal at the base camp to transport the cargo—which included the transponder itself. The rest of the team would then unload the portal as quickly as they could and Swenson would send the transponder, and the divot, back. Using the portal this way was risky, but it was the only practical way to move a significant volume of produce six thousand miles.

The chief problem was that they had no reliable location reference for the reverse transport. It wasn't as simple as just sending it back where it came from. The spatial relationship between the two endpoints hadn't changed much, but in the time that had elapsed the planet had rotated around its axis and its sun, and both moons had rotated around the planet. These celestial motions resulted in distortions of the gravity field in the region between the two endpoints. The impact on the portal technology was not insignificant.

The transit portal leveraged a novel understanding of physics that translated a spherical volume, in zero time, from one place to another. The amount of power required was proportional to the volume of the transfer and the square of the distance between the endpoints. They had a portal, but only a small fraction of the power that would be necessary to send themselves back across fifty-seven light-years to Earth. The portal there, with its much larger power source, would have to initiate that transaction. But moving things around on the planet wasn't so much a problem of power as of precision.

It is a common misconception that no two objects can occupy the same space at the same time. This is not so much a law of physics as it is a natural consequence of other principles. Reality is that whether you look at how atoms fit together to make molecules, or how subatomic particles fit together to make atoms, or how quarks fit together to make subatomic particles, the empty spaces are many orders of magnitude larger than the constituent objects. You really could interleave the particles of one rock into the space occupied by another.

In the next instant, however, mayhem would ensue. The original rock had achieved a delicate balance between the four fundamental forces of nature: gravity, electromagnetism, the strong force, and the weak force. The sudden introduction of a large number of new particles within the same space would dramatically upend that balance, with unpredictable consequences.

The portal's solution to this dilemma was to preamble the transfer with a rapidly expanding void that would push out whatever matter currently occupied the destination. This still has significant consequences for anything currently occupying that space, but if mostly air, the implications are trivial.

In the two iterations they had executed the day before, the first return transport had been off by nearly three inches and the second by more than two in the opposite direction. This left an arc-shaped gap on one side of the divot, and packed and mounded soil on the other side where the portal had pushed away whatever was in the space to make room for the incoming sphere.

Swenson and Sakhr seemed to think this would be okay so long as they were working in soft soils, but they couldn't be sure what would happen if they got into hard rock where pushing it away had potentially seismic consequences. That was why Swenson had sent the drone ahead and marked the spot where he wanted the transponder.

Guerrero set the four-wheeler down. Grass covered the floor of the clearing. As Culpepper saw it up close she realized animals had grazed here, and fairly recently. Memories of growing up on the farm and racing through the cow pasture crept up unbidden from somewhere in her mind. She quickly shoved them back into their closet and barred the door.

"Watch your step. There are landmines everywhere."

Guerrero had been about to step out of the vehicle, but jerked back and spun around to look at her.

She smiled and pointed through the windshield at the ground in front of the vehicle where the grazers had left behind the byproducts of their craft.

Guerrero shook his head, then climbed out. He grabbed the transponder from the back of the four-wheeler and walked toward the drone. She watched him go for a few steps before he stopped and turned around.

"Are you coming?" he asked.

"Do I have a choice?"

"No. We've been through this. We don't need to do it again."

We're wasting time, She thought. *You don't need my help to set up the transponder, and I don't need your help to start assessing vegetation.* But she said, "Right behind you." She got out of the vehicle, grabbed her pack, and followed after Guerrero.

The transponder sat atop a tripod. Guerrero set it up directly below the hovering drone and adjusted the height to position it five feet off the ground.

He looked at his watch. "We have an hour and twenty minutes until the communication window opens. Where to?"

Culpepper hitched up her pack and started walking toward the treeline. Guerrero followed, and the drone drifted up above the treetops and shadowed them. Swenson had programmed it to track them and monitor their perimeter for potential threats.

The drone didn't bother her. She knew the threat of aggressive wildlife was real, and having advance warning of potential predators made her feel a lot more comfortable. That was part of why she didn't feel the need to put up with Guerrero and all his paranoid rules.

For the next hour they collected samples of everything they could find that might have nutritional value. Culpepper tagged and cataloged them so if anything proved promising they could find more of it. Finally, Guerrero said, "We'd better get what we have back to the staging area. They'll make radio contact in about five minutes. We need to be ready to transport."

Culpepper piled the last of what she was looking at onto the sled that Guerrero had fashioned from an animal skin and tree branches. He started dragging it back toward the clearing.

She followed, but began lagging further and further behind. When Guerrero got far enough ahead that she didn't think he could hear her footfalls, she slowed to a stop. When he kept going, she turned and headed off in another direction.

Now we stop wasting time. Meathead can deal with the transport. I'll get started surveying the next quadrant around the clearing.

Rebellion

Guerrero checked his watch as he dragged the sled into the clearing. "Two minutes. We're cutting it close, but we'll make it."

When Culpepper didn't respond, he turned and looked back over his shoulder. All he could see was grass and trees. He dropped the sled and activated his radio.

"Dr. Culpepper, where are you?"

He kept watch on the treeline, but couldn't see very far into the forest.

"Dr. Culpepper, please respond."

He was about to race back into the trees when he heard the radio activate.

"Beachhead to Forager. How do you hear?" It was Decker's voice.

He looked back toward the transport staging area, still fifty feet away.

"Forager to Beachhead. Loud and clear."

"Are you ready to ship?"

"Negative, Beachhead. Give me a couple of minutes."

He picked up the sled again and pulled it as fast as he could the rest of the way, quickly unloaded it, and then ran back toward the treeline, dragging the sled with him. In theory, the transport out would be very accurate. In practice, he didn't want to take any chances of getting sliced in half by being too close to the translated sphere.

When he got to the treeline he dropped the sled. "Forager to Beachhead. Ship it."

Guerrero blinked and it was gone.

"Shipment received, Forager. How are things going there?"

He turned and started trotting back into the forest. "I have a problem here. Dr. Culpepper got away from me. Can you establish control over the drone and use it to help me find her?"

The voice on the radio changed. "I'm on it." That was Swenson, the engineer.

Guerrero kept going in the direction he had come but slowed his pace. If she had stopped along the way, he should have found her by now.

"I think I have her south and east of your current position. It's hard to see through the trees, and she's near the limit of the camera's resolution."

Guerrero had just turned to face southeast when he heard the loud crack of a gunshot. He bolted in the direction of the sound, pulling his rifle from his back and disengaging the safety. "Sitrep. I just heard a handgun discharge."

Steadman's voice came over the comm. "She's running now, in your direction. We can't see yet what she might have fired at. Suggest you veer five degrees to your left for intercept."

Guerrero heard another gunshot as he adjusted his path, swerving between the trees at a full run.

"One hundred yards. She's being chased through the trees by what looks like a moose. It's gaining on her. You're not going to have a shot. The moose is going to get there first. Engaging Plan C."

Guerrero pushed harder. Plan C was an idea he had proposed three months earlier when Commander Steadman and Dr. Zindell were in similar predicament— being stalked by a large bear. The idea was to try to crash the drone into the animal to take it out. They hadn't used it then, in large part because the likelihood of success was low. Chances weren't any better now. At best it would buy him a few seconds. But maybe that would be enough.

He heard another gunshot and adjusted course again. Suddenly, he saw Culpepper running straight at him. She was firing blindly over her shoulder, not even trying to aim the weapon. The moose was right on her heels. Steadman was right. There was no way Guerrero could hit the moose without hitting Culpepper, and the moose would get to her before he did.

He heard an ear-splitting shriek as Plan C shot out of the sky and crashed into the moose's antlers. The moose crashed to the ground, but he quickly picked himself up and resumed the chase.

"Forager, we've lost video. Say your status."

Guerrero didn't hear the request. His attention was focused on one thing, and one thing only. As he and Culpepper approached each other, he waved for her to keep running, tossed his useless rifle aside, and ducked behind a tree. Culpepper raced by him, the moose closing within a few feet behind and still focused on Culpepper. As it stormed past Guerrero's tree, he lunged and managed to get a grip on one antler.

Guerrero yanked the moose's head around, forcing it off its pursuit of Culpepper. He used the force of the exchange to lever himself up onto the animal's back. Grabbing the other antler, he pulled back on the moose's head, causing it to rear up on its hind legs. When it came back down, it used its powerful neck muscles to throw Guerrero forward.

"Forager, please respond."

Guerrero lost his grip as he sailed over the antlers. He tried to position himself to land with a shoulder roll, but another tree interrupted his trajectory. A loud crack and searing pain announced the failure of his femur as he crumpled to the ground.

Out of the corner of his eye, he saw the moose charging toward him, antlers down. Ignoring the pain in his leg, he rolled away from the tree to free his sidearm. In one smooth motion he drew the weapon, pointed it at the top of the approaching animal's head, and fired.

The moose's legs collapsed beneath it, but its forward motion continued as it skidded into Guerrero. He managed to get both arms up to block the antlers, but the corresponding shove sent another torrent of pain through his leg and pinned him back against the tree.

Fighting to remain conscious, he activated his radio. "Beachhead, Forager. We may have a problem."

Revisit

Culpepper continued to run, driven by absolute panic. She had no doubt the moose was faster than her, and little confidence that Guerrero would be able to stop it. Expecting at any instant to be knocked off her feet by antlers crashing into her back, she flinched and nearly lost her stride when she heard a gunshot ring out behind her.

Daring to glance back over her shoulder, she saw no pursuit. She stopped and turned to get a better look. *No sign of the moose.* She bent over with her hands on her knees and struggled to catch her breath.

He did it!

She activated her radio. "Thanks, Alex. Are you okay?"

Panic revisited as seconds passed without a response. Then she remembered she'd turned off her radio shortly after sneaking away from Guerrero earlier.

She turned it back on and was about to repeat her question when she heard Decker's voice. "Beachhead to Forager. We've lost video. Say your status. Please respond."

She knew Decker was trying to talk to Guerrero, so she waited for him to respond.

"Beachhead to Forager. Please respond."

Culpepper broke into a full run. "Culpepper here … stand by."

"What's going on, Doctor?"

She managed to squeeze out between breaths: "Moving back … last known … position. Let you know … when I get … there."

She saw the antlers first. Then she saw Guerrero's motionless torso tangled between them, his lower body twisted at an unnatural angle wedged between the animal and a tree.

"Alex!"

His head came up, but he couldn't turn far enough to see Culpepper's approach.

"It's about time you got here. I was beginning to think you were going to run all the way back to base."

She punched him in the arm. "What were you thinking!"

Guerrero looked up at her with a forced grin, intense pain evident on his face. "You *told* me to stick to my strengths. Now you want me to *think*, too?"

Decker's voice came over her comm. "What's your status, doctor?"

"He's alive and conscious. Appears to be in a lot of pain. There's a lot of blood here, but I think it's from the moose, not him."

26

Guerrero waved at her head. "Let me have your headset."

Her first instinct was to tell him to use his own headset, but she managed to bite her tongue before the words came out and handed it to him.

"Guerrero here. Tango is down. I have a broken left femur, probably a compound fracture. A couple of sore ribs, probably only bruised. Drone is sour. My radio is sour. My tablet is sour. Everything else is sweet. How much window do we have left?"

"Three minutes," Decker said.

"I need to talk to Teri again," Tornquist said.

"Do it," Decker said.

Guerrero pulled the earbud out and handed it back to Culpepper. She wiped it down with her shirt before putting it back in her ear. "Culpepper here."

"Teri, we're going to lose communication in just a couple of minutes. I need you to work quickly. Can you tell if there's any bleeding or open wounds in the vicinity of the fractured upper leg?"

Culpepper quickly worked her way around to the other side of the moose where she could see Guerrero's legs. The right leg disappeared underneath the massive carcass. The left one had an unnatural bend in the middle of the thigh that she hadn't noticed when she arrived. Guerrero winced as she felt around the girth of his leg for signs of blood soaking through his clothes. "Sorry," she said softly.

She activated the radio. "No sign of bleeding, but definitely broken at about the middle of the length of the bone. The lower half deflects about ten degrees from the upper half."

"Okay," Tornquist said. "It could be worse. You're going to have to straighten that and find some way to put a splint on it. Then you're going to have to keep him off his feet for the duration. Not even hobbling around on one foot. Horizontal. You stay with him until the next window opens. I'll try to get some—"

The radio went silent. Culpepper felt the tendrils of panic reaching for her again. "Get some what! Say again!"

With every heartbeat the tightness in her chest grew stronger. "Beachhead, this is Forager! Please respond!"

Guerrero winced again as he stretched to touch her arm. "It's okay. Mabel just orbited out of range. We're on our own for the next ten hours and twelve minutes while she swings back around. That's plenty of time to get everything fixed and get back on our game. Just breathe."

She took a deep breath and let it out slowly. "Okay. The doctor said we need to straighten this out and then splint it." She got up and stood by his feet. "I expect this is going to hurt you more than it hurts me."

She reached for the foot, but Guerrero held up a hand. "No!"

She felt sympathy for him. The reality that she had caused this threatened at the edge of her conscience. She pushed it back, knowing that if she let it in right now, it would overwhelm her.

"I'm sorry, but it has to be done."

He forced a smile again. "Yes. But if we do it now, we'll just have to do it again after we extricate me from my buddy here." Guerrero patted one of the antlers. "We have a bigger problem, potentially. All this blood is like a pair of golden arches erected above the highway. Every hungry critter for miles around is going to converge here expecting a free lunch."

Culpepper was incredulous. She waved at the moose. "How can you worry about a trophy at a time like this!"

Guerrero laughed—and cringed when his ribs reminded him they were injured too. "I'm not worried about a trophy. As much as I'd love to gift this animal to Dr. Zindell, and salvage this meat to help get the team through winter, and have this hide to make a couple of better winter coats, none of that is going to happen. In this heat, the meat will already be unfit for human consumption before the next communication window opens. We might salvage the hide, and maybe a DNA sample, but my concern is for my life. I don't want to still be pinned underneath him when the whole neighborhood shows up to see what's on the menu. That's what we have to fix first."

She felt chastened. "What can I do?"

He waved at the moose. "Straddle his back and grab the antlers. Pull back as hard as you can to try to lift the head. If you can get it up enough, I'll pull myself out."

Culpepper looked at the moose, then back at Guerrero. She straddled the animal's back and pulled back on the antlers with everything she had, managing only to lift the nose a couple of inches.

Guerrero struggled to pull himself out, but couldn't budge. "It's no good. Let it back down."

As gently as she could, she set it back down. "What's wrong?"

"My right foot is up under his shoulders. I was afraid that might be the case. There's no way you'll be able to move him enough to get me loose."

She felt panic encroaching again, a tsunami of guilt not far behind. She grabbed the antlers and pulled as hard as she could, trying to use her legs to get additional leverage. Guerrero wasn't even trying to extricate himself. Instead, he was looking up at the trees.

"At least try to help! We can't just sit here."

Guerrero looked at her. "We're not going to just sit here. You're going to go back to the clearing and get the four-wheeler. Then you're going—"

"I'm not going anywhere. Dr. Tornquist said I had to stay with you. We'll figure something out."

"I know what she told you, and I know why. And she's right, at least given her limited understanding of our predicament. She's a doctor, and I'm not. I'm the guy who knows how to survive. And right now, survival is what's at stake. There are two paths forward."

Guerrero pulled out his KA-BAR knife and laid it on the animal's back. "You can take this knife and start carving this animal into small enough pieces that you can move it off me. I would guess that will take you about twenty minutes—if you have the stomach for it. And all the while, the scent of blood will be building in the air. Then, once you get me out, you'll have to drag me, with both of us soaked in blood, all the way back to the clearing. Please don't take this the wrong way—I'm not trying to be disrespectful, I'm trying to be objective and rational—I don't think you have the capacity to drag this much dead weight that far. Especially not while fighting off any predators that might come along and want to take *your* trophy."

Culpepper tried to cool down. She hated to admit it, but he was right. And he was way ahead of her in thinking through their options.

"What's the second path?"

"You go back and get the four-wheeler. We can use the winch to pull the moose away. Then we can load me into the back seat and fly back to the clearing."

"And what keeps you safe while I'm gone."

"Oh, I won't be safe. That's part of why I need you to run every step." He pulled out his pistol and laid it beside the knife, then pointed back over his right shoulder. "You should find my rifle in the grass ten or twenty yards back that way. I'd appreciate it if you could fetch it for me before you go."

Culpepper looked around. She wasn't happy about it, but she didn't have any better ideas. She walked back in the direction Guerrero pointed, found the rifle and brought it to him.

"Are you sure about this?" she asked.

Guerrero checked the rifle. "Do you have any better ideas?"

She shook her head.

He nodded toward her handgun, holstered on her belt. "How are you fixed for ammunition?"

She drew the gun and pulled the clip. "One in the chamber and three in the clip."

"Spare clip?"

Culpepper grimaced. He'd told her on multiple occasions that she needed to carry a spare clip. It had seemed like dead weight to her. Before today, she'd never fired it except for target practice. Now she wished she'd listened.

Guerrero drew one of his spare clips and tossed it to her. "Put the full clip in the gun. Keep the partial in reserve."

She looked at Guerrero. "What about you?"

Guerrero smiled. "I have two more full clips, and this one only one round down." He patted the moose on the head, reminding her where the one round had gone. "Plus the rifle and the knife."

Culpepper turned toward the clearing. She heard Guerrero behind her say, "Teri, this will buy me time; it won't get me out of here. You're my only ticket out."

She set her chin toward the clearing and ran.

Relax

Guerrero watched her disappear among the trees.

Ten minutes for her to get to the four-wheeler, then another five to get back here. Depending on how much difficulty she has finding me. And assuming she doesn't run into any other problems on the way.

He studied the surrounding landscape, looking first for any sign of predators or scavengers that might be approaching, but also to understand his blind spots and get a better sense of where they might come from if they did. A slight breeze wafted from right to left. The clearing was to the right. The scent of the dead moose was blowing left.

That's where they're most likely to come from.

He slowed his breathing as he listened for threats. A howl echoed in the distance to his left. He guessed it was at least a quarter mile away.

Not good. I hope she gets back here soon.

As the minutes passed with no visible signs of predators, he was beginning to think this might all work out. He checked his watch.

Ten minutes. She should be in the clearing by now.

Something moved to his left. He brought the rifle to his shoulder and looked through the scope. An animal that looked like a wolf had stopped and was looking right at him.

I can handle one wolf.

As he watched, another wolf came up through the trees behind the first and stood beside it. Then a third. Within a few seconds he counted fifteen, noses sniffing the air as they stalked in his direction. There might have been more. It was hard to see through the trees.

That could be a bigger problem.

A gunshot rang out in the distance behind him. The wolves stopped their approach and looked in the direction of the clearing. Two more discharges in rapid succession.

Pretty soon this is going to be a fair fight. God, watch over her.

The scope read the wolves at a thousand feet. After another thirty seconds of silence, the wolves resumed their approach, spreading out as they stalked their prey.

I was really hoping they wouldn't do that.

If they encircled him, it would be a lot more difficult to defend against them, and it would make it harder to scare them off. Bunched up, if he could take a couple of them out it might make the others rethink their plan. Spread out, most of them would never know how many of their pack had already gone down. He'd end up having to kill, or at least try to kill, every one of them.

He took careful aim at the one he'd seen first—presumably the leader of the pack. *Eight hundred feet.* He gently squeezed the trigger.

As the crack of the rifle shot echoed through the forest, most of the wolves stopped and perked their ears. The leader went down yelping loudly, a mangled shoulder rendering its right foreleg useless. Guerrero had aimed for the center of its head, a clean kill shot. He hadn't intended to maim the animal, but the reality was that his miss probably saved the lives of several other wolves. The pack's attention was drawn to their yelping, foundering leader, who was desperately trying to retreat on three legs. Soon the rest of the pack fell back as well.

Sorry, bud. I know you were just doing your job.

A sudden commotion in the trees overhead startled him, and he swung his rifle around to point in the direction of the disturbance. He held fire as he saw the four-wheeler descending through the treetops, breaking off some of the larger limbs as the smaller, more flexible branches dragged against the sides of the vehicle, leaving deep scratches and creases in the side panels. As Culpepper spun around to point the tailgate and cargo winch toward the moose, Guerrero noticed the rear side window on the driver's side had been shattered.

Can't wait to hear that story.

She released the winch and jumped out of the cab. Grabbing the end of the cable, she hurried over to the moose.

"Wrap it around his neck, as low over the shoulders as you can get it," Guerrero said.

As she worked the cable around the animal, she said, "Looks like things were quiet here."

"Yeah. I can't remember the last time I could just sit outdoors and relax and enjoy the peaceful sounds of nature."

After she secured the cable to the moose, she pulled out her tablet to remotely access the winch controls. "Here goes." She drew the line taut and then slowly lifted the front half of the animal off Guerrero's leg.

Guerrero pulled his right leg out and then quickly scooted himself across the ground to get clear of the moose and the tree. Excruciating pain in his broken leg left him fighting for consciousness. Through gritted teeth, he said, "Okay. You can let it down and unhook, but leave the winch cable out for now."

"Why? What are we going to do now?"

He gestured toward the winch cable as she unhooked it. "That's Plan B. Plan A is for you to find at least three good sticks, each at least eighteen inches, as straight as you can find them. And make sure they're strong. While you're doing that, I'm going to pull myself over beside the four-wheeler."

She moved toward him. "Let me help."

"You are helping. I can do this myself, probably with a lot less pain than with you trying to drag me. What I can't do as well as you is forage for splints. We need to get this splinted before we try to load me into the vehicle."

She started collecting broken branches. "What's Plan B?"

Guerrero rolled onto his stomach, wincing as his broken left leg shifted. He put his elbows forward, his rifle cradled in his forearms, and leveraged himself closer to the vehicle. His eyes grew wide and his face went pale as his left foot caught on a rock. He gritted his teeth against the pain and rested his forehead on the ground, pushing back against a wave of nausea.

"Stay put," Culpepper said. "Let's get that splinted before you try to move any further."

"We don't have time for that," he said as he pushed his elbows forward again. "Plan B is what we do if I lose consciousness. With or without the splint, there's a good chance that when we try to get me up into the vehicle, I'll pass out. If that happens, you have to use the winch to load me up into the bed of the truck and then warp out of here. Get back to the clearing. Wrap the winch cable around my chest, under my arms. Don't try to wake me up, don't try to splint the leg, just get us out of here."

Guerrero pulled himself forward another foot.

"What are you so worried about. You said it's been quiet here."

He thrust his arms forward but wasn't yet ready to drag the leg again. "No. *You* said it's been quiet here. I said I couldn't remember the last time I had a chance to relax." Guerrero nodded toward the woods in the direction where he'd shot the wolf. "I counted at least fifteen wolves out there, hunting as a pack. One of them isn't coming back. The others are. I just don't know when."

Culpepper looked panicked, almost dropping her sticks as she looked into the distance.

Guerrero heaved himself forward.

She looked back at him and said, "Will these work?"

Guerrero looked up. "Yeah." He pulled a multi-tool from his belt and tossed it at her feet. "Now take the saw and trim them up. Cut the longest one to about four feet, the other three to about two-and-a-half. The long one needs to stretch from my rib cage to my calf. The others from just below the hip to the calf."

Culpepper knelt down beside the four-wheeler and started trimming the sticks. Guerrero slid forward another foot. The pain was getting more tolerable, but he knew that wasn't necessarily a good sign. His body would release endorphins to alleviate the pain to allow him to continue to function in a crisis, but it didn't mean the injury wasn't still real—and maybe getting worse.

Rescue

Culpepper's arm was already getting tired. She shook it out and started sawing into the second stick.

This is not *my fault. I didn't do* anything *wrong. All I was trying to do was my* job.

She didn't believe that now any more than last thirty-seven times she'd thought it.

"So what happened to the window?" Guerrero asked.

Culpepper cringed and kept her eyes on the stick in her hand. "I don't know. It looks like someone broke in. The eight-track is missing too."

Guerrero laughed, and then grimaced. He pulled himself forward again.

Culpepper finally looked up. "Why didn't the drone warn me about the moose?"

Guerrero shifted his elbows forward again. "Two reasons. When you separated from me, the drone was forced to take up a position between us to keep an eye on both of us. The further you got from me, the further it got from you. The canopy of the trees compounded the problem. The moose was on the other side of you, even

39

farther from the drone, so the drone couldn't see the threat until it was almost on top of you."

Guerrero pulled himself forward again. "Second reason —if I'm not mistaken, you had your radio turned off again. Your tablet relies on your radio data channel for distances of more than a few dozen feet."

She shook her arm again. "Decker's going to kill me, isn't he?"

Guerrero suppressed another laugh. "Only if we don't make it back alive." He edged forward again. "This is all collateral damage. We knew we were putting people and materiel at risk when we started this mission."

As Guerrero pitched his elbows forward again, Culpepper noted he seemed to be making faster progress with less pain.

Maybe things are improving.

He paused, propped up on his elbows, and looked up at her. "Life is fatal. Everything that lives, dies. We knew when we came to this planet we were risking death. But even if we hadn't come, all of us would still have died. Eventually. Each of us judged that it was a risk worth taking for the hope of what we might find when we got here."

Guerrero turned his eyes back to the four-wheeler. He pitched his elbows forward and then used them to drag his body twelve inches closer to safety.

"This mission is no different. There were risks either way, whether we huddled in our warm boxes, slowly starving as we waited for the snow to melt, or flew off into the unknown in search of greener pastures."

He looked at her again. "In both cases, there was really ever only one choice. You're here because you knew that."

Tears flooded her eyes as guilt choked her. "But the drone ... your leg ... all *this!*" She slammed the side of her fist into the fender of the four-wheeler, creating yet another dent. "I caused it *all!*"

She was sobbing now. A faint voice in her head reminded her they were not out of trouble yet, and she needed to get back in the game. She tried to focus on the voice, but the torrent of guilt was overwhelming.

"All I wanted was to do my job. I'm good at my job. Why can't people see that I don't need help?"

Guerrero had finally reached the side of the vehicle. He pulled himself up to a sitting position and leaned back against the rear door. "Have you ever ridden a horse?"

The question caught her off guard. It took her a moment to understand what he'd asked. "Yes."

"Do you like horses?"

She wiped tears from her eyes. "Yes. What does that have to do with anything?"

"When you ride a horse, do you disrespect the horse? Think it's weak?"

"No! Of course not. They're beautiful animals. Powerful animals. Intelligent animals."

"Humble animals," Guerrero said. "That horse you ride is the definition of humility. Being humble is not being weak; it is harnessed, disciplined, controlled strength. The horse comes to believe that it can be more successful partnered with the human than going it alone. The rider is not stronger or faster than the horse; he brings a different kind of strength to the partnership. Together they can do things neither could do alone."

She clipped another twig off the splint she was shaping. "And I'm not humble." Is was part question, part statement.

"And you're not humble. You're the wild horse, so worried you'll be disrespected or exploited that you refuse to be harnessed; unable to see how much more you could accomplish joined to a team."

She bristled at his presumption, but was shocked by the sound of applause from the voice in her head. This man had risked his own life to save hers. And that after she had willfully flouted his rules—rules she could now see were only intended to keep her safe. Now he sat here with a broken leg, enduring a level of pain she couldn't even imagine, and yet refusing to condemn her. Speaking truth. And that it was truth she had no doubt.

She set the last splint in front of him and used the sleeve of her shirt to wipe her face. "Will those work?"

"Yes. Now get the rope from my pack. Then fasten the winch cable around my chest."

"But you're still conscious."

"Yeah, but I may not be after you start lifting my leg to wrap that rope around it. It'll be easier to get the cable around my chest while I'm conscious and sitting up than while I'm out cold lying down."

As she wrapped the winch cable around his chest, hooking it on itself in front.

"Now wrap the rope loosely three times around my chest, under my arms."

She grabbed one end of the bulky spool of climbing rope and measured out about thirty feet. She picked up Guerrero's knife to cut it.

He lurched toward her, the knife just out of his reach. "No!"

She paused, the edge of the blade poised against the cord. "What? I'm just cutting off a piece long enough to bind the splints."

Guerrero dropped his hand and gritted his teeth, taking several deep breaths as he waited for the pain to pass.

"That's an irreplaceable resource. There's only one more like it anywhere on the planet, and no way we could make another that would even begin to replace it. You can't *uncut* a climbing rope."

She dropped her hands to her side, one still holding the rope and the other the knife. "This *rope* is more important to you than your *life*?"

Guerrero started to laugh but instead rubbed his bruised ribs. "No, it isn't. But that's a false choice. We don't have to cut it to save my life. Just spool up the excess, and I'll carry it with me until we can work out a better solution."

She shook her head but handed the knife to him and recoiled the rope. She hefted the awkward bundle. "How long is this?"

"Sixty meters. About two hundred feet."

Culpepper started unrolling the rope again.

"What are you doing *now*?" Guerrero asked.

She let out about fifteen feet and then laid the rest on the ground. Fishing out the other end of the rope, she said, "Thinking. That's what *I* do." She pulled another fifteen feet of the other end out from the center of the spool, then looped it once around the rest of the bundle to hold everything together. Then she took the first end and used it to wrap once around the other side of the coil.

That left her with a large coil of rope, tied in two places to keep it bunched together, with two fifteen-foot spans hanging out on either end. She laid the long splint on top of it and tied one of the lengths, right where it came out of the coil, to the stick about a foot from one end. Then she took the other section of rope and tied it to the middle.

She laid the assembly beside Guerrero.

He looked at it. He looked up at her and said, "You're pretty good at that."

"What?"

"Thinking."

Culpepper smiled and nodded appreciation for the compliment. His decency made her want to start crying again, but she thrust the emotion aside and knelt beside him to start binding the splints. The rope toward the short end of the stick she wrapped around his rib cage, leaving the end loose.

"Why tie one end of the splint to your torso? This is going to make it hard for you to move."

"Yes, but hopefully this will help keep the leg immobilized. Even bending at the hip will put stress on the fracture that could cause it to dislocate. We'll try to work out a better solution later, but this will have to do for now. Help me swing my legs around so I can lay down."

Culpepper grabbed his feet, using the good leg to stabilize the bad one. She gently lifted his legs and then guided them around as he spun on his hips.

He blanched. "I'm so sorry," she whispered as he lay down. She tightened the loops around his rib cage and tied the rope off to the upper end of the stick.

"So which of us is the horse, and which is the rider?"

Guerrero stifled a laugh in a vain effort to protect his bruised ribs. "Every metaphor breaks down at some point. We're not the horse and the rider. We're Chief Petty Officer Alejandro Guerrero and Doctor of Botanical Science Teresa Culpepper." He looked her in the eye with a smile distorted by pain. "And we make a great team."

She picked up the next splint. Compassion colored her face as she looked at him and said, "This may hurt." She lifted his broken leg and when she wrapped the second length of rope twice around it, his body went limp. Her instinct was to drop what she was doing and try to awaken him, to make sure he was okay, but she could hear his instructions echoing inside her head. He *wasn't* okay, and waking him up wouldn't make things any better —for either of them.

She quickly slid the other two splints inside the two loops of rope on the front, back, and inside edge of the leg. Trapping his ankle under her arm to hold the leg up off the ground, she wrapped the rope around the splints before tying it off by the ankle.

She reached to slap his cheek when she heard a low growl off to her left. She turned to see one of his wolves not twenty feet away, staring right at her with its teeth bared and growling. Her heart raced as her eyes counted the predators spread in front of her. Her mind muddled in a haze that seemed to prevent rational thought as her ears registered more growls coming from behind.

No! She cut through the wave of panic, grabbing her tablet and activating the winch. After vaulting herself over the sidewall of the vehicle, she switched to the vehicle remote navigation controls, and as soon as she saw the winch cable draw tight she elevated the four-wheeler as high as she could without crashing into the forest canopy.

She drew her handgun and rushed to the side where the winch was pulling Guerrero up. A lone wolf charged toward them. Guessing it was going to leap at Guerrero dangling below the vehicle, and fearing it might still be able to reach him, she sighted in on the animal's head. Just as it launched, she squeezed off a shot.

Rescue

It was the first time in her life she'd actually hit what she aimed for.

Regroup

Guerrero sat sideways in the back seat of the four-wheeler, his broken and splinted leg propped up beside him. They had re-established communication with Beachhead a couple of hours earlier when Mabel made another pass overhead. Dr. Tornquist had used the portal to send over a portable X-ray scanner, medical grade splints, and painkillers. He hadn't taken any medication yet and didn't intend to if he could avoid it. He needed to stay coherent until they were out of danger, and in his estimation, they weren't. By several days.

Culpepper had X-rayed his leg and, with direction from Tornquist, reset the bone and resplinted it. Now he could bend at the waist.

They sat silently, eating a dinner of MREs. Neither complained, despite the atrocious taste, understanding the sacrifice the rest of the team had made sending their entire remaining supply of the nutrition-packed rations to provision them for the mission. They had plenty of food left at the base camp, but there were still a few nutritional requirements—primarily vitamins—they hadn't been able to source locally. Now they had to not only find food compatible with human physiology, but they also had to find solutions for those nutritional gaps made worse by sacrificing all their remaining MREs.

As Guerrero finished off his dinner, he stared at the shattered side window of the four-wheeler. His jacket now covered the opening, the door frame trapping the garment in place. They would have to wait to see how the patch would hold up when they started for home at cruising speed, but it would work for tonight to keep critters from joining their camping trip.

"What happened to the window?"

Culpepper was sitting in the front passenger seat, reviewing Tornquist's analyses of the produce they had shipped this morning. She didn't answer.

He tapped her on the shoulder. "What happened to the window?"

"What?" She didn't look up. "What window?"

"Don't give me 'What window?' That window!" Guerrero gestured toward it, even though she wasn't looking his direction.

"Oh ... that window." She kept looking at her tablet. "I may have shot it out ..." Her voice trailed off.

"I'm sorry, I didn't hear that last part. Could you say that again?" He was starting to enjoy this.

She thrust her tablet into her lap with a huff and looked up at the windshield, still not daring to look at him. "I shot out the window. There. Are you happy now?"

Guerrero guffawed. "What? Did you lock your keys in the car?"

"There was a huge … bird … vulture looking thing … perched on the roof of the four-wheeler. I didn't have time to mess with it, so I shot it."

"A bird? With a pistol? Shot it, or shot *at* it?" It was only the memory of his bruised ribs that kept him from laughing.

"Obviously, I hit the window. But I scared it away."

"So those other shots I heard?"

She finally turned to look at him. "When it flew up, it flew straight at me. I had to fire several more shots to finally scare it away. I'm glad you find this so amusing, but I remind you: you're the one who told me to 'run every step.' You should also bear in mind that there was, in fact, a pack of wolves preparing to make brunch out of you. I got the job done, the fastest way I knew how."

He knew she was right. It wasn't fair to expect her to address the problem the same way he would have, or to demand his level of marksmanship from her. He held up his hands in surrender. "You're right, and I'm sorry. I very much appreciate what you did—everything you've done. I know this hasn't been easy for you."

Wolves howling in the distance caused them both to look in the direction of the sound. They could see nothing but moonlit grass and a distant treeline.

"Will they come back?" she asked anxiously.

"Probably not. At least not tonight. Our moose friend was more than a feast for them. They're howling now because one of their number didn't make it home. They're sending up a beacon in hopes of leading him back to his pack."

She turned back to look at him. "You don't think they'll want to avenge his death?"

Guerrero shook his head. "No. They're wolves, not humans. Vengeance isn't in their makeup. They may know he's dead; they may just think he's missing. Either way, it's unlikely that they even connect that with us. I was eight hundred feet away when he went down. An adversary with that kind of reach is a completely foreign concept to them."

She turned to look out the windshield. "Two."

Guerrero looked at the back of he head. "I beg your pardon?"

"Two of them went down." The words caught in her throat as she remembered killing the animal. "I had to shoot a second wolf as we were escaping."

He couldn't see her face, but he could hear the tears in her voice. His father had taught him to hunt when he was a young teenager. He still remembered what he felt when he killed his first rabbit. He had looked forward to it— dreamed of it—for weeks. But when he saw the animal go down, he felt none of the excitement or sense of accomplishment he'd expected. He felt a lump in his throat, and something inside him wept for the life he'd taken.

It was a teachable moment, and his father had used it well. *"Son, we don't do this for sport. We do this for food.*

Sometimes it's necessary to kill an animal. Sometimes it's necessary to kill a person. But don't ever expect to find joy in the act. May God have mercy on your soul if you ever do."

He'd killed many animals since—two today—but always for a reason, and never with joy.

He reached forward and put a hand on her shoulder.

"Why did you do it?" she asked.

"Do what?"

She wiped her face with the sleeve of her jacket. "Take on the moose. I knew the rules; you explained them to me repeatedly. I willfully chose to break them." She turned around and looked at him. "I deserved to suffer the consequences. It wasn't your responsibility."

"But it was. It's what I do. It's who I am, who I was created to be."

She hung her head.

"What was your dream?" he asked.

She raised her head. "What?"

"My mom once told me that a lack of humility is always rooted in insecurity. In your case, I'm betting you had a dream—and a team you believed was going to help you achieve it. Your team let you down, so now you're out to prove you don't need anyone else—that you can make it on your own. Am I right?"

She took her jacket off and rolled it up to make a pillow, then pulled a blanket up from the floorboard and spread it over herself as she stretched out across the front seat.

His question went unanswered.

Relate

Culpepper stared out the windshield as the alien sun broke over the horizon, the uneaten half of her breakfast MRE in her lap. She didn't see the sunrise, or the trees, or the clearing. She saw golden fields of alfalfa, her father's old blue tractor pulling the harvester, dumping bales of hay behind. She could smell the freshly cut sheaves.

What was my dream?

She heard Guerrero stir in the back seat. "Good morning."

"Morning," he said groggily.

She handed his MRE over the seatback. "Breakfast?"

He took the packet and tore into it. "Thanks."

"I grew up on a farm," she started hesitantly. *Can I do this?* She could hear the packaging crinkle as Guerrero took a bite of his breakfast.

"My parents were farmers. I have two brothers. We grew up helping Mom and Dad in the fields."

She had to pause. *I don't think I can do this.* She took a deep breath. *Catharsis.* It hurt, but somehow it felt right.

"All I ever dreamed about was growing up to be part of a farming family." She wiped a tear from her eye, then felt Guerrero's hand on her shoulder.

"What happened?"

"I went to college to study agriculture. In my second year, Dad was diagnosed with cancer. By the end of the year, he was gone."

She paused again, taking several deep breaths.

"I was always a daddy's girl. His death crushed me, but I thought, 'We're still a family. We'll get through this. We'll continue his legacy.' I came home that summer expecting to help with the harvest. Instead, I learned that my mother and brothers had decided to sell the farm. My mother didn't think she could do it without him, and my brothers had no interest in spending their lives 'working in dirt.'"

She looked down at the floor. "I was devastated. Betrayed. I went back to school, but I was adrift. Without a farm—or family—to go back to, agriculture made no sense. I decided to change my course of study, but all I knew was farming, and all I could think about was my dad. So I decided to focus on immunology and oncology. Somewhere along the way, I hit on the idea of combining that with my agriculture background by researching botanical solutions for diseases."

She turned to look back at Guerrero for the first time this morning. "And here I am."

Guerrero gave her shoulder a gentle squeeze before sitting back in his seat. "That's the toughest thing about families: growing up. If you're blessed to grow up in a strong family like you and I were—"

"*I* didn't grow up in a strong family," she hissed. "I had a strong father. The rest of them were cowards and back-stabbers."

Guerrero stared back with a questioning look. "Do you really believe that? Or is it just possible that you weren't the only one crushed by your father's death? Have you ever thought about what your mom was feeling?"

A venomous response leapt forward in her mind, but another part of her stopped to consider a question she realized had never occurred to her. *What was that like for Mom?*

"For you, the farm was your dream," Guerrero said. "It was a dream you could still achieve, with your mother and brothers to help you achieve it. But what was her dream? Could the farm help her live it, or would it serve as a continual reminder that her dream was dead and buried, never to walk again?"

The realization of the pain her mother must have experienced, and her own oblivion, overwhelmed her. She began to sob, wondering if she'd ever get the chance to make things right with her mom.

She felt Guerrero's hand on her shoulder again. "Teri, you had no more right to expect your mother and brothers to give up their own dreams to help you chase yours than they would have had to expect you to give up yours to pursue theirs. But there's nothing wrong with your dream. You can still achieve it. You just need to find the right team."

Recall

"Forager, this is Beachhead. How do you hear?"

Guerrero, still consigned to the back seat, motioned to Culpepper to activate the four-wheeler's radio.

"Beachhead, Forager. Read you loud and clear."

"How was your night?" Decker asked.

"I don't know. I slept right through it. You'll have to ask Dr. Culpepper."

"He snores," Culpepper said.

Guerrero looked at her with mock disappointment, folding his hands over his wounded heart.

"We're ready to get back to work," he said. "We're almost a day behind schedule. That's a lot of ground to make up."

"Not so fast, macho man," Dr. Tornquist interjected. "The X-rays look good. Dr. Culpepper did a good job setting the break, but you're not ready to get back up on the moose just yet."

"Everyone's a comedian. What is this? Roast Alex Day? And no one told me about it?"

"I'm going to cook your goose if you reinjure that leg," Tornquist quipped.

Guerrero decided to change the subject. "What's the verdict on yesterday's morning shipment?"

An uncomfortable silence met the question. Guerrero looked at Culpepper. She was reading something on her tablet, presumably Tornquist's detailed reports, her face twisted up in confusion.

"That's the good news," Tornquist said. "It looks like two of the fruits you found yesterday are edible and should close our nutritional gaps."

Culpepper bounced in her seat, her face beaming.

Decker said, "Commander Steadman and Dr. Sakhr are working to provision another mission to come out and pick up where you left off."

The statement caught Guerrero by surprise. He bit his tongue. He needed to count to ten before he spoke.

"You've both done a fantastic job," Decker said. "Pack up and head for home. We'll coordinate flight plans so you can rendezvous with Forager Two on your way back."

"With all due respect, sir," Guerrero said—not really feeling it—"that's an unnecessary waste of valuable resources. By the time we get home, we'll have drained three-quarters of this four-wheeler's power reserve. If you send a second mission, that'll deplete most of a second vehicle. And a second drone. We still have no idea how much longer we'll be on our own on this planet."

Recall

Commander Steadman came on the line. "Alex, under normal circumstances I'm sure Dr. Culpepper would be up to the task of harvesting the food we need. But these aren't normal circumstances. We have to regard this as a hostile environment. You have no drone to monitor a perimeter, and you're in no condition to guarantee her safety."

Guerrero glanced at Culpepper, who was now staring at the radio in the dashboard with tears welling up in her eyes.

"Give us today. Twelve hours," Guerrero said. "I have an idea how we can make this work."

"Alex—" Decker started.

"Twelve hours. If we don't deliver this evening, we'll pack up and head for home at first light. We'll give you new X-rays tonight. If Dr. Tornquist isn't happy, we'll bug out."

Guerrero and Culpepper looked at each other apprehensively as the silence stretched.

"Dr. Culpepper?" Decker said.

"I trust Alex to keep me safe. And you can trust me to keep him honest. Twelve hours. That's all we ask."

The silence was agonizing. Guerrero knew Decker was discussing it with Steadman and Tornquist. There was only one right answer. But would they trust him?

Relaunch

"Are you sure about this?" Culpepper asked as she helped Guerrero ease himself out of the back seat. They were both wearing climbing harnesses. His made it easier for her to support him.

"Well, to be honest, this is the riskiest part of the plan. For the next fifteen feet, you're going to be driving."

She punched him in the shoulder.

"Ouch!" He looked at her with mock confusion, then grinned. "That's not what I meant. Getting me into the bed of the vehicle without injuring my leg is the risky part. Hand me the big stick."

She pulled the long stick that had been part of their improvised splint out of the back seat and held it up in front of his face. "I meant what I said about keeping you honest."

He smiled. Tipping his head in salute, he accepted the stick from her. He stood away from the truck, balancing himself on his one good leg and the crutch.

"Now, I need you to shift the vehicle away and spin it around so the bed faces me. Then gently edge it back so I can roll onto the tailgate."

She climbed into the cab and activated the controls.

Did I really beg for this?

As she slowly backed toward him, he suddenly fell over. She jumped out of the cab and raced around to the back. "Alex!"

He looked up at her from the tailgate where he lay. "What?"

She chastised herself for the emotional response. *What did you expect it to look like when he 'rolled onto the tailgate'?*

"That was perfect," he said. "Now if you could help me shift my legs around the other way. I think I could do it myself, but it will put less stress on the break if you help."

They positioned him so his head and right shoulder were hanging off the edge of the tailgate. Then they used the rope to secure his climbing harness to several different anchor points around the bed.

"Now give me your tablet, and swing the winch out over the right side of the bed. Then attach the winch cable to the back of your harness."

After she attached the cable to the harness she felt the winch take up the slack. Guerrero was using her tablet to control it.

"The next thing we have to do is get your climbing harness adjusted properly," he said. "Right now it's configured to favor orienting you upright. We need to lower the anchor point to very near the center of mass of your body. That will allow you to hang horizontally. By shifting your arms and legs, you'll be able to control your orientation from head-up to head-down."

"How do we do that?"

"Slowly lean forward, shifting your weight from your feet to the harness. Keep your body straight, bending your knees or elbows to shift your center of mass. If you can easily float level to the ground, we're good. If you can't touch the ground with your hands, the harness is too high. If you face-plant, the harness is too low."

She bent her knees and lifted her feet. She tried to pitch forward but couldn't. "It doesn't work. I can't lean forward at all."

"We expected that. That's the way we always configure a harness for an inexperienced climber. Stand up and take the load off the winch line, then adjust the attachment point lower. Just go an inch at a time. It's easy to overshoot."

She adjusted the harness and tried again. "Still not there, but I can tell the difference. I'm adjusting again."

After the fourth adjustment, she nearly hit her head on the ground when she lifted her feet. "Okay. I think I overshot." She struggled to right herself.

"Good. Go for a final position midway between the last two adjustments. Before you test again, attach that canvas bag to the front of the harness."

She attached one of the bags they had been using to collect produce to the anchor point. When she shifted her weight from her feet, she found that she had good control over her pitch.

This is kind of fun. I could get used to this.

"Okay. I think that's got it. Just one more question."

"What's that?"

"What does this have to do with picking fruit?"

She suddenly felt a tug on her back and saw the planet lurch away from her. She screamed.

"Sorry about that," he said after they stopped about twenty feet off the ground. "Forgot to adjust the sensitivity on the altitude control. Now I'm going to lower you down far enough that I'll be able to see you from where I'm hanging over the edge of the tailgate."

She saw the ground slowly rising to meet her.

Did I really say I trusted him to keep me safe?

She noticed that as she descended, she was also slowly rotating. She tried to turn back, but couldn't figure out how. "Problem. I can control tilt, but not rotation."

"Yeah. It'll be a challenge. When you get into position over the trees, you'll be able to use the branches for leverage to turn yourself as necessary to reach the fruit. The thing we have to watch out for is when we raise you back up. You'll need to keep an eye on the four-wheeler as you ascend and push against the bottom of it to reorient yourself. The closer you are to upright and vertical, the easier that should be."

Culpepper practiced moving her arms and legs, trying to adapt to how her arm motions affected her orientation.

"Are you sure about this?" she asked.

"It's the best idea I have. You can pick fruit without setting foot in the forest. There shouldn't be any predators of significance in the treetops. At least no wolves or moose ... mooses ... meese. From here, I can navigate the vehicle and control the winch to get you into position and keep an eye on the surroundings for anything we need to worry about. I also have a good position to offer cover fire if necessary. Are you up for this?"

"Moose," she said.

"What about them?"

"They're moose. The plural of moose is moose. The word is invariant."

Guerrero smiled at her as she dangled below. "Oh."

Culpepper looked down at the twenty-foot drop below her.

Tell me again how the riskiest part of this is getting you onto the tailgate?

She looked back up at Guerrero. "Yeah. I'm good. Let's stop wasting daylight."

Return

Guerrero sat sideways in the back seat, his broken leg propped up in front of him. He couldn't see well from this position, so he had Culpepper's tablet linked to the four-wheeler's cameras and was using it to scan the terrain below.

"There they are!" Culpepper shouted, struggling to be heard above the roar of wind blowing past the shattered window. "Two o'clock. About a mile up ahead."

"Are you sure that's the same herd?"

"There's no way of knowing. We didn't tag any of them. And horses aren't particularly territorial. It's not uncommon for more than one herd to graze the same area. But it doesn't matter. I just want to see horses again before we get back to our igloos."

The facilities at their base camp were hardly igloos, but he understood what she meant. After three weeks living out of a pickup truck, he was actually looking forward to getting back to their small encampment. Still, this was the last they would see of sunshine and warm weather for several months. Back at camp, almost two feet of snow covered them and they didn't have any reason to expect that to melt before spring.

Culpepper nudged the four-wheeler in the direction of a small prairie that interrupted the savanna. She brought the vehicle in slowly, tangent to the perimeter of the herd. Before setting down, she spun around so the tailgate faced the horses.

Guerrero opened his door and worked himself out of the back seat. It wasn't an easy task to accomplish without stressing the fracture, but sitting in the same spot for the four-day journey home just wasn't going to happen. He had to get out and move the rest of his body. By the time he'd gotten his good leg out, Culpepper had come around to help. She got under his shoulder and helped him lift himself out, then retrieved the pair of crutches Guerrero had fashioned for himself out of tree limbs.

They made it around to the back and dropped the tailgate. He slid on and then pushed himself back just inside the bed, leaning back against the sidewall for support with his broken leg stretched out in front. Culpepper sat on the other side, her legs dangling and her hands gripping the edge.

They watched the horses in silence for a few minutes.

"Have you noticed how there are always a few of them watching while the rest ignore us and eat?" Guerrero asked.

Culpepper smiled at him. "Every herd needs its protectors."

Guerrero returned the smile. "Thanks, but that's not what I was getting at." He motioned toward the horses. "Watch them. Keep an eye on the ones that are watching us and see what happens."

Culpepper turned back to look at the horses. "What am I watching for?"

"Anything. Everything."

"That one just stopped watching and went back to grazing."

"Keep watching."

"Two more just stopped ... there goes the fourth. So?"

"So how many were watching when you started counting?"

"Five. Why?"

"And how many are watching now, after four of those five stopped?"

Guerrero watched the side of Culpepper's face as she studied the horses.

"Four," Culpepper said. She turned to look at Guerrero. "What of it?"

"Five minus four equals four? They're taking turns watching us. It isn't that a few horses are more paranoid than others, or that some are assigned to stand watch. They take turns. That way everyone gets to spend most of their time grazing, but there are always a few watching for danger."

He looked back at the horses. "What I haven't been able to figure out is how they signal each other to hand off responsibility."

She laughed. "We're sitting here looking at these beautiful animals against this awesome landscape, and you're trying to figure out how to defeat their security system."

Guerrero smiled at her. "Occupational hazard." He looked back at the horses. "Anticipating the future."

Culpepper followed his gaze back to the horses. "How so?"

Guerrero reached into a crate beside him and pulled out two of the fruits they had collected. He tossed one to Culpepper. "It depends on how long we're stuck on this planet. The mission plan was a maximum of three months, and that presumed that we had an uninterrupted supply line. We have no way of knowing when, or if, rescue will come. These four-wheelers won't last forever. By the time we get back to base, ol' red here will be seventy-five percent depleted. A few good horses could help us a lot with getting around our home turf and maybe with planting more expansive gardens in the spring. That would take some of the load off the four-wheelers and extend their life for things the horses can't do."

He took a few bites out of his apple, then threw the half-eaten fruit in the direction of the herd. It landed a few feet from one of the horses standing watch.

They both watched as the horse walked over and sniffed the fruit. It took a bite and chewed, its gaze remaining fixed on the two interlopers and their odd conveyance. Two more chomps finished the snack. The horse lifted its head toward them and neighed. Guerrero took another whole fruit out of the crate and tossed it at the animal's feet. It took a bite, and while it chewed, two of its friends came over and ate the rest.

When the first horse raised his head again, Guerrero took another apple out of the crate but held it out instead of throwing it. The steed stamped its foot and whinnied. Guerrero motioned with the fruit for the horse to come and get it. After a few seconds, it turned back into the herd and resumed grazing—its two friends following behind.

"You didn't really think it would be that easy, did you?" asked Culpepper.

"No, but you have to start somewhere."

They settled back to watch the horses for a few more minutes. Guerrero was about to suggest that they get back on the road, so to speak, when he noticed a tear on Culpepper's cheek. "What's wrong?"

"Nothing." She wiped the tear.

He was pretty sure it wasn't "nothing," so he decided to give her a few more minutes with the horses.

"For three months," she said, "ever since the first moment when I arrived on this planet, every time I looked at the horizon I saw the farm of my childhood." She wiped her face with her shirt-sleeve. "I've trained myself not to look there because the memories were so painful."

She turned to face him, not bothering to try to hide the tears. "Today, for the first time, when I look at the horizon, I see what I could do with that space. A farm. A greenhouse. A ranch. A research lab. Everywhere I look is another opportunity. So many opportunities, I could spend the rest of my life here and not scratch the surface."

She turned back to look at the horses. "In the few short days she was here, Pam had already seen it. 'Benignitas,' she called it. Bountiful opportunity. It took me three months to get it. I'm ashamed to say what went through my mind when she first suggested the name."

Guerrero's gut wrenched at the mention of Pam's name. He still felt a degree of responsibility for her death in the first week of the mission. He knew it wasn't rational—there was no way he could have anticipated the act of treason that would claim her life—but it was his job to get her home safe. He knew Pam Weaver would never make that journey. The only comfort he had was in the knowledge that death was not final; he knew where she had gone, and that he would follow her there when his own time came.

But now was not the time to revisit that failure. Now was about the turmoil Teri was experiencing. He edged himself forward and slid off the tailgate, standing on his good leg and leaning against the vehicle. He put an arm around her shoulder and pulled her close. She lay her head on his shoulder as they sat in silence.

"Thanks for letting me stop here." She looked up at him. "And thanks for not giving up on me."

Return

He looked down at her and smiled, giving her shoulder a gentle squeeze. "C'mon. Let's go home."

Afterword

This short story may have left you with unanswered questions. Where are they? How did they get there? Why are they stuck there? Why is this planet so much like Earth?

If you'd like to find answers, pick up a copy of the full-length novel *Two*, by Steve Swaringen, from your favorite bookseller. You'll also encounter more challenging questions, like how did *we* get *here*? Are we stuck here? Why is life on Earth the way it is?

Learn more at SteveSwaringen.com/Forager.

Acknowledgments

Life is a team sport, and writing is no different. I couldn't have done this without the support of several people who have volunteered, in ways big and small, to be part of the team.

Guerrero's insights into humility and teamwork are heavily influenced by Patrick Lencioni's book, *The Ideal Team Player.* If you want to learn more about being a team player, I highly recommend the resource. (Actually, I highly recommend pretty much anything Patrick Lencioni has written.)

The careful reader may notice that most (if not all) of John C. Maxwell's *The 17 Indisputable Laws of Teamwork* are demonstrated (though not articulated) in the story. That isn't because I intended to model them so much as because they are, pardon the repetition, indisputable. I highly recommend the book to anyone who wants to take their team to the next level.

I sincerely appreciate the support of the Rockwall Christian Writer's Group (RCWG). Their constructive critique and heartfelt support have made me a better writer, and this a better story.

In particular, I'd like to thank two RCWG members, Sue Anne W. Kirkham and Vernon R. Goodman, who read early drafts of this story. Sue Anne W. Kirkham is a freelance writer who blogs at yourrecipesforlife.com. She has published magazine and newspaper articles as well as online profiles of courageous everyday people of faith. If you enjoyed the story, their radical candor made it what it is. If you didn't like it … well … that's all on me.

I'm especially indebted to my wife, without whose patient forbearance I could not do this.

Other Books by Steve Swaringen

If you'd like to learn more about the adventures of Alex Guerrero, Teri Culpepper, and the rest of their team, you can find it at SteveSwaringen.com.

The first book in the series, *Two*, tells the story of mankind's first leap into interstellar space and the second planet in the universe to see human footprints. A team of ten scientists and support personnel is sent through a dimensional portal to explore what appears to be a vibrant garden in the depths of space. Is life there compatible with humanity? Is there intelligent life there? Could we colonize the planet? Why does it look so much like Earth?

Forager (this story) follows in the aftermath of *Two*. The team has been cut off from Earth. No supplies, no communication, no way home. No idea what happened that prevents them from connecting to the portal on Earth. Those who have survived this long are by no means out of danger.

One (a work in progress at the time of this writing) explores what is happening on Earth (the *first* planet in the universe with human footprints) that has caused the link to be broken.

Look for these books at your favorite online retailer, and keep an eye on SteveSwaringen.com to learn about new installments in the *Benignitas* and *Forerunner* series.

About the Author

Steve Swaringen is a husband and father living in Rockwall, Texas. He earned a Bachelor of Science degree in Electrical Engineering from Texas A&M University, College Station.

He believes passionately that if our faith is true—that God created this world—real science cannot help but point the way to the real God.

To learn more, visit SteveSwaringen.com.

www.ingramcontent.com/pod-product-compliance
Lightning Source LLC
Chambersburg PA
CBHW070535130626
46555CB00003B/1437